LONDON'S
Greatest Kid

Written by Karla Courtney
Illustrated by Cinta Villalobos

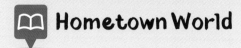

Hometown World

This headline's just in...
Top news, it's the latest!
Read all about it,

We've found

London's GREATEST!

This **MARVELLOUS** kid
Is the best through and through,
So now let me share
All the cool things they do.

They're **CUDDLY**
and **THOUGHTFUL**,
And hug like a bear.
From *Greenwich* to *Lambeth* –
They'll always be there.

The **FUNNIEST** monkey you'll find at the zoo...

A great cheerer-upper when you're feeling blue.

A **CURIOUS** bunny,
They want to know more...
"Where did this come from?"
"What's this by the door?"

EGYPTIAN MUMMY

GUIDE BOOK

And "WHEN CAN WE EAT?"

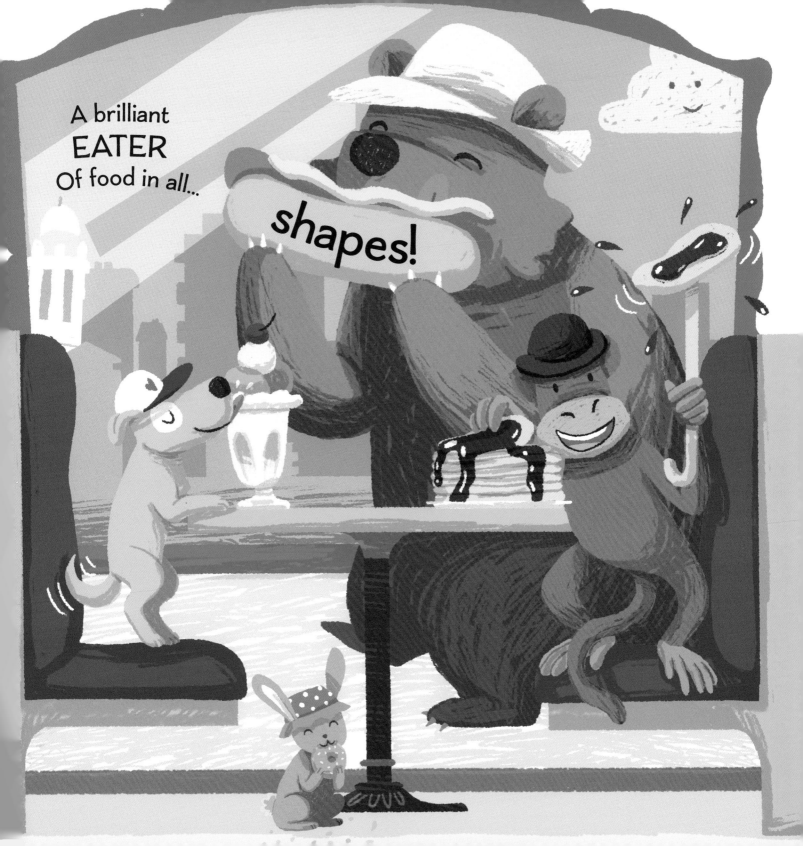

When facing their fears
They might find things frightful,

THAMES RIVER TOURS

Then out ROARS a lion
So BRAVE and delightful.

PRIDE OF THE THAMES

And even when things get
A little bit hairy,

They laugh, "This is awesome –
The Thames isn't scary."

This wise little owl's
Remarkably CLEVER,
They find their way through
Almost any endeavour.

They're whizzy with numbers,
Can solve any sum.
"I'll take five of these, please,
They're perfect for Mum."

Flo's Fancy Flowers

2 FOR 1

5.10

A real human rhino,
This kid is so STRONG –
Nothing's too heavy,
Too large or too long.

BUS STOP

TIMETABLE

Westminster Abbey

Tower of London

Canary Wharf

Wembley Stadium

They **NAP** like a sloth
And can snooze anywhere.
Victoria or *Euston*...
They really don't care.

Piccadilly Embankment Trafalgar Sq Westminster Tower Bridge

(And sometimes when things
Don't quite follow the plan...
We know that this kid's tried
The **BEST** that they can.)

As SWEET as a kitten –
This kid is *so* CUTE.
They're CHARMING
and LOVING
And GENEROUS to boot.

From *Southwark* to *Camden*,
They've rushed here and there,
They've shown someone special
Just how much they care.

So, there now you have it,
This kid is the best.
They're FRIENDLY and FUNNY
And BRAVE... and the rest.

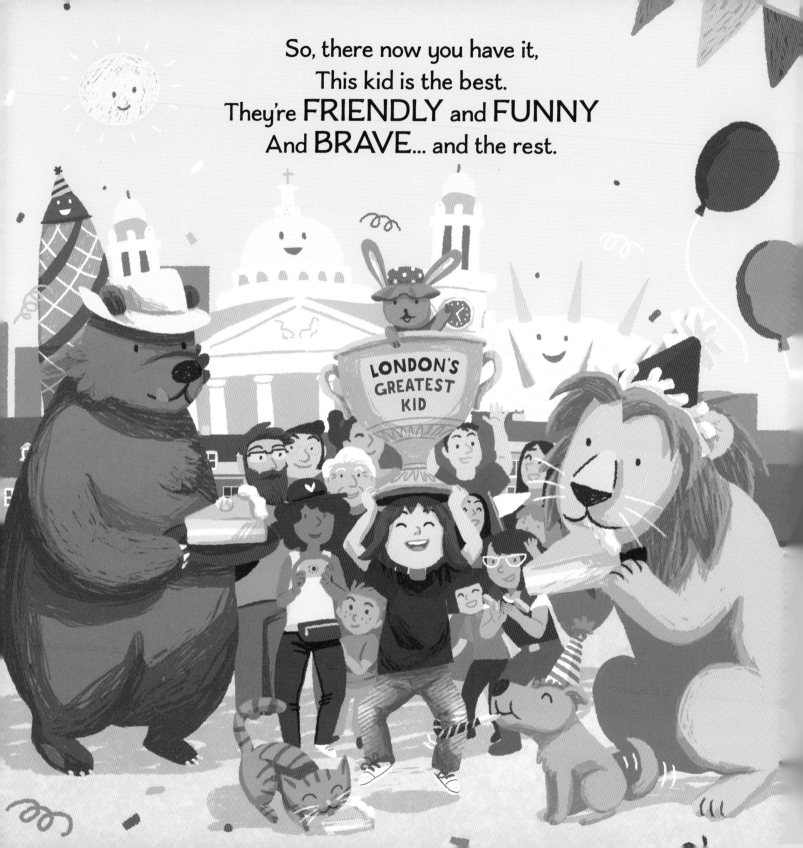

You've heard all about them...
You know what they do...
The GREATEST in *London*?

Well, that kid is...

For Marshall, my greatest kid – K.C.

Written by Karla Courtney
Illustrated by Cinta Villalobos
Designed by Geff Newland

First published by HOMETOWN WORLD in 2018
Hometown World Ltd
7 Northumberland Buildings
Bath
BA1 2JB

www.hometownworld.co.uk

Follow us @hometownworldbooks